W9-AUY-344

This edition published by Parragon Books Ltd in 2015
and distributed by

Parragon Inc.
440 Park Avenue South, 13th Floor
New York, NY 10016
www.parragon.com

Copyright © Parragon Books Ltd 2015
Text © Hollins University

Written by Margaret Wise Brown
Illustrated by Marilyn Faucher

All rights reserved. No part of this publication may be reproduced,
stored in a retrieval system or transmitted, in any form or by any means,
electronic,mechanical, photocopying, recording or otherwise, without the
prior permission of the copyright holder.

ISBN 978-1-4723-7817-0

Printed in China

all the little Fathers

PaRragon

Bath · New York · Cologne · Melbourne · Delhi
Hong Kong · Shenzhen · Singapore · Amsterdam

All the bear fathers were catching fish with their children.

All the dog fathers were giving their children bones to chew.

All the grasshopper fathers were jumping over their children.

All the squirrel fathers were
hiding nuts for their children.

All the lion fathers were
roaring with their children.

All the monkey fathers

were hanging out with their children.

All the giraffe fathers were helping their children reach up high.

All the bird fathers were bringing
food to their hungry children.

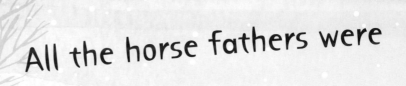

All the horse fathers were

leaping with their children.

All the cat fathers were
purring to their children.

All the rabbit fathers were hopping

home with their children.

All the little fathers were
putting their children to bed.